A PUFFIN BOOK

PROPERTY OF

_____

_____

CATHERINE STORR was born in 1913. She was educated at St Paul's Girls' School in London and then at Newnham College, Cambridge, where she read English Literature. Although her ambition was always to be a writer, she decided to study medicine and went on to work as a psychotherapist. Catherine was married in 1942 and in 1944 had the first of her three daughters. She returned to her writing and created short stories for her young daughters, including the adventures of *Clever Polly and the Stupid Wolf*, which has remained in print ever since it was first published in 1955. Catherine wrote more than thirty much-loved books for children and young adults, which have been translated into many different languages. She died in 2001, aged eighty-seven.

Books by Catherine Storr

CLEVER POLLY AND THE STUPID WOLF
POLLY AND THE WOLF AGAIN
TALES OF POLLY AND THE HUNGRY WOLF
MORE STORIES OF CLEVER POLLY AND
THE STUPID WOLF

CATHERINE STORR

MORE STORIES OF CLEVER
POLLY
AND THE STUPID
WOLF

Illustrated by Jill Bennett

A PUFFIN BOOK

PUFFIN BOOKS

UK | USA | Canada | Ireland | Australia
India | New Zealand | South Africa

Puffin Books is part of the Penguin Random House group of companies
whose addresses can be found at global.penguinrandomhouse.com.

puffinbooks.com

Originally published under the title *Last Stories of Polly and the Wolf*
by Faber and Faber Limited 1990
Published in Puffin Books 1992
Reissued under the title *More Stories of Clever Polly and the Stupid Wolf*
in this edition 2016
001

Set in 13.5/20.5 pt Sabon LT Std
Typeset by Jouve (UK), Milton Keynes
Printed in Great Britain by Clays Ltd, St Ives plc

A CIP catalogue record for this book is available from the British Library

ISBN: 978-0-141-36924-2

www.greenpenguin.co.uk

Contents

1. The Wolf at School   1

2. Thinking in Threes   17

3. At the Doctor's   32

4. In Sheep's Clothing   48

5. You Have to Suffer in Order
   to be Beautiful   66

6. Kind Polly and the Wolf in Danger   78

1. The Wolf at School

POLLY was on her way to school one morning, when she found the wolf trotting beside her. There were a great many other people around, so she was not particularly frightened, but she was curious.

'Where are you going, Wolf?' she asked.

'I'm going to school,' the wolf replied.

'My school?' Polly said.

'Of course, your school. Isn't it the best round here?' the wolf asked.

'Much the best. But Wolf ... if you're thinking you'll be able to get to eat me in school, you'll be disappointed. There are always crowds of us all together. If you tried to eat me, you'd get caught and probably shot. Or something.'

The wolf wasn't listening. 'Crowds? Of plump little girls? Of good, juicy little boys? Like this lot here?' he asked, looking round at the pavement covered with children hurrying towards the school gates.

'You won't have a chance to eat any of them,' Polly said, answering what she knew was in the wolf's mind.

'Hm. Pity. But I don't know why you are always thinking about food. That's not what I am going to school for. My mind is on higher things,' the wolf said virtuously.

'Higher than what?'

'Higher than my stomach. Brains, you stupid little girl. I am going to school to develop my brains. I am going to school so that I can become clever. Even cleverer than I am already,' the wolf added hastily.

2

'Who told you school would make you clever?' Polly asked.

'Read it in the paper. There was an advertisement. DO YOU WANT YOUR CHILD TO BE SMARTER THAN ANYONE ELSE'S? START EARLY LEARNING LESSONS NOW. I know you have lessons at school, and as I haven't got a child it seemed meant for me. I shall stay in your school until I can outsmart you, Miss Polly. Then, when I've eaten you up, and perhaps a dozen or so of these other children, I shan't need to learn any more and I shall leave.'

By now they had reached the school gates, and the other children were squeezing their way through. 'I don't think you can just walk in and join in the lessons without asking,' Polly said to the wolf, as they stood outside, left to the last.

'You must introduce me. Go on! If you're so clever, you can think of some way of getting me in. If you don't . . . Grrrrrr,' the wolf said, showing his teeth.

Polly looked round and saw that they were alone. 'All right. I'll try,' she said, and they went together across the playground to the cloakroom door.

'Good morning, Polly,' said Miss Wright, but when she saw Polly's companion, she said quickly, 'You know we don't allow pets in the classroom. Your dog must go home. Immediately!'

'He's not a dog. He's a friend who's come to stay with us from abroad. To learn English,' Polly said quickly, while she whispered to the wolf, 'Get up on your hind legs and try to look like a friend from abroad.' Beside her she could hear the wolf growling. 'Dog! Pet! Never been so insulted in my life!'

'He's very large. Isn't he too old for this class?' Miss Wright asked.

'He's big for his age,' Polly said.

'He's very dark. And hairy.'

'He's foreign. He doesn't speak the language very well yet. If he could sit next to me, I could help him,' Polly said, thinking it would be better not to let the wolf sit next to Susie, who was the plumpest girl in the room, or next to Freddie, who might tease him into behaviour unbecoming to a pupil in Miss Wright's class.

'Foreign? How interesting. What country does he come from? What are you, dear?' Miss Wright asked the wolf. Polly wondered if he had ever been addressed as 'dear' before. His answer was indistinct, and Miss Wright looked puzzled for a moment, then she said, 'Hungary! Well now! I don't think we've ever had a child from Hungary in our school before. We must all do our best to make you feel at home.'

'I'd feel at home quicker if I could have something to eat,' the wolf muttered.

'What's that, dear? I didn't quite catch what you said.'

'He says he's feeling the heat,' Polly said.

'Really? You could take off your coat, if you're feeling too warm, dear. Now let's all get out our exercise books, shall we, for our first lesson? Numbers!'

'Take off my coat? Doesn't she know it's my skin?' the wolf said, a little too loud.

'What was that you said?' Miss Wright enquired.

'He said his coat is quite thin,' Polly said out loud.

'And what is your friend's name?' Miss Wright asked.

'Wol– Wolly,' Polly said, having had no time to think up anything better.

'We don't like nicknames in this class. I shall call him by his proper name, Walter. When you speak to me, Walter, you must call me Miss Wright. Do you understand?'

'I will not be called by a stupid name like Walter!' the wolf said, very loudly indeed.

'What did you say?' Miss Wright asked.

'He says he wants a drink of water,' Polly said.

'Then he'll have to wait until the lesson is finished. I can't have you all running in and out whenever you feel like it. Now, we really must get on with the lesson. Let's see who can add up quickly, shall we? Who can tell me what ten and ten make?' Miss Wright began. Sally put her hand up, ready with the answer, but before she could speak, the wolf said, 'Ten what?'

'Do you know the answer, Walter? Good . . . good boy. What is it then?'

'Ten what?' the wolf repeated.

'It doesn't matter what. It's just a number, dear. Ten anything,' Miss Wright said.

'Of course it matters what. Ten buns would be good. Ten little pigs would be better. Ten fat little girls like that one would be better still. Only I haven't got a freezer, they'd be difficult to store. I'll settle for the pigs,' the wolf said.

'I don't know what you're talking about, dear. Perhaps they do numbers differently in your country. So we won't worry about buns or pigs, will we? So what do ten and ten make?' Miss Wright repeated.

'Twenty,' Polly said quickly. Numbers was one of her best subjects.

'She didn't put her hand up! I was going to say twenty!' Sally complained.

'I'll give you another question, then. What is twenty-four divided by eight?'

Sally took a little time to think about this. But the wolf had heard one of his favourite words. 'Who ate it? What did they eat?' he asked.

'Walter, didn't you hear me tell you that you must say "Miss Wright" when you speak to me? And I didn't see your hand go up, either,' Miss Wright said.

'Five,' Sally said.

'No, that's not right. Very well, Walter, you tell us. Twenty-four divided by eight.'

'Was it the ten little pigs?' the wolf said.

'I wasn't talking about pigs.'

'Did they eat the buns?' the wolf went on.

'Three,' Polly said, loudly, hoping that Miss Wright would not hear this remark.

'What is three supposed to mean? Oh! Yes. Eight into twenty-four. Quite right, Polly. Now, who can tell me what seven and six make?'

By the end of the numbers lesson, the wolf was confused, Miss Wright was cross and Polly was exhausted. 'I don't think that can have made you any cleverer,' she said as they put away their books and got ready for the play they were rehearsing for the end of term.

'I've never heard such nonsense! What use are numbers if they aren't fastened to something? You don't see five or three or a hundred just floating about in the air. If she'd said five sausages, or three apples or a hundred beans, I'd have understood what she was getting at. It could even have been interesting. Now what do we do? Isn't it time for school dinner yet?'

'Not nearly. Miss Wright's going to give us our parts for the school play.'

'What's the play about? If it's about little Red Riding Hood, I could act the wolf. I bet I'd do it much better than any of these silly little creatures,' the wolf said hopefully.

'It isn't Red Riding Hood. It's Hansel and Gretel. There isn't a wolf in it, so I don't know if Miss Wright will let you have a part.'

'I know that story! They get lost in a wood, don't they? I'm sure there must have been a wolf in that wood. Woods in fairy stories always have wolves in them.'

'This one didn't. It had a witch who lived in a gingerbread house.'

'Why gingerbread? Nasty stuff. It makes my throat tickle.'

'To catch children who liked it. Then she cooked them and ate them.'

'That sounds like a good part. I shall be the witch.'

Polly thought this was unlikely. But when Miss Wright was distributing the parts, no one else, except a very small boy called Eric, wanted to act as a witch, and at last Miss Wright was forced to notice the large black paw which had been waved every time she offered the part to another child, who turned it down. 'You want to be the witch, Walter? Are you sure you can manage it? She doesn't have much to say, but . . .'

'She catches children to eat,' the wolf said.

'Don't worry, dear. You can be sure that our story has a happy ending, though of course I don't know how you may have heard it in Hungary.'

*

'Well, Wolf? Now you've had a whole day in my school, do you feel clever? Cleverer?' Polly asked as they came out of the gates at the end of the afternoon.

'Much cleverer. That story we were acting was an inspiration to me. In fact, I think I'll skip school tomorrow. I have some urgent business to attend to in another direction,' the wolf said, and, rather to Polly's relief, he hurried away.

It was a few days later, that, on her way home from school, Polly saw a curious construction standing shakily in the road near to her own home. It looked like a badly put together garden shed, made out of brown paper. Windows and doors were drawn on the paper. Some sticky tape fastened a candy bar on one wall. On another was written a message:

THIS HUSE IS MAD OF G JINJEBRED

Polly stood still to examine it. She had an idea that she knew who had put it there and who was likely to be inside it. While she was looking, the building shook violently, there was a tearing noise, and the paper of one of the windows burst open.

'Who's there?' said a voice.

'Me. Polly,' said Polly.

'A little girl? Lost in the wood?'

'I'm not lost and this isn't a wood. But I am a girl.'

'That's the important part. Have a candy bar,' said the voice.

'There's only one,' Polly said.

'It's for you.'

'I'm not sure . . .' Polly began, but before she could finish, the door of the house had been wrenched apart, and the wolf stood there, grinning at her horribly.

'Got you! I knew you'd never be able to resist a candy bar,' the wolf said.

'I haven't had it yet,' Polly pointed out.

'Hurry up, then. You eat that first, then I'll take you home with me and put you in my oven, like the witch did to Gretel. At last!' the wolf said, happily.

'I thought you didn't like gingerbread,' Polly said.

'Hate it. The gingerbread was for you, not me. What I'm looking forward to is a good roast dinner. Roast girl.'

'You haven't read your fairy stories carefully enough. Don't you know what happened to all those children the witch roasted in her oven? They didn't turn into roast child, they turned into gingerbread,' Polly said.

'I don't believe you!' the wolf cried.

'Have a look at the play. I've got it here, because I'm learning my part,' Polly said, offering the book to the wolf, who looked quickly at the end, snarling with disappointment.

'It's a cheat! It can't be true! Do you mean to say, Polly, that if I roast you now, you're going to become a gingerbread girl? Like these pictures in the book?' the wolf asked.

'I should think so. It seems to be the rule when you catch someone with a house made of gingerbread and sweets,' Polly said.

'But I don't like gingerbread!' the wolf cried.

'I'm afraid that's all you're going to get,' Polly said.

'It isn't fair! That woman who taught us said the story ended happily! This isn't a happy ending!' the wolf moaned.

'I don't think she meant it would be happy for a wolf. Too bad. You'll have to think of something else, won't you? See you at school on Monday?' Polly called as she quickly made her escape. But somehow she didn't think the wolf would be coming back to school to make him clever enough to catch even cleverer Polly.

2. Thinking in Threes

'HOW DID they do it? Goldilocks just walks in at the front door, without being asked, and if they'd remembered to bolt the bedroom window, they'd have got her. And I can't get Polly to my house without all the trouble in the world, and then I've never managed to keep her there,' the wolf said to himself, closing the book of fairy tales in which he had just read, for the twentieth time, the story of the Three Bears.

He thought deeply. Was it because they were bears, and not wolves? No. Goldilocks didn't know who lived in the house when she found it. She must have been hungry, that was why she'd gone into an empty house to eat their porridge. 'Easy-peasy. All I've go to do is to get some porridge,' the wolf thought. No sooner thought than done. He fetched his basket and set out for the shops.

'A pound of porridge,' he said to the man behind the counter.

'Sorry, sir, we don't sell porridge. Oats, sir,' the man said.

'Oats? I'm not a horse.'

'No, sir. I can see that you're not a horse. I didn't mean to be rude, sir. Oats is what porridge is made of. Very easy, it is. You just boil oats in water.'

'And that makes porridge?'

'Yes, sir. Instructions on the packet.'

The wolf took the packet and read the instructions. Making porridge did indeed seem easy. He bought two packets in case his efforts with the first did not prove successful, and went home very much pleased with himself. 'Aha, Miss Polly! I'll have you eating in my house very soon – and eaten soon, too,' he said to himself.

A day or two later, Polly was passing the end of the street where the wolf lived, when she smelled a really horrible smell. She looked along the road and saw a trickle of smoke coming out from under his front door. She ran as quickly as she could towards it, and arrived just as the door was thrown open, and a gush of smoke and a slightly singed wolf leapt out.

'Wolf! What's the matter? Is your house on fire?' Polly panted.

'What? Who? No, no. No cause for alarm. I just left something to cook for a little too long. Why, it's Polly!' the wolf said, wiping black paws on a black apron.

'Smells terrible. What were you cooking, Wolf?' Polly asked.

'Nothing particular. Porridge, that's all. Porridge,' the wolf said.

'I thought you didn't like porridge?'

'Hate it. Looks like putty, tastes like mud and feels . . . Ugh!' the wolf said.

'Then why . . . ?'

'For a visitor. Which reminds me. I suppose you wouldn't care to come in and have a bite to eat, Polly?' the wolf asked, very sweetly.

'No, thank you, Wolf.'

'I could make the other packet.'

'Is that going to be porridge too?'

'How did you guess? I probably wouldn't burn it this time.'

'I'm really not hungry, thank you, Wolf.'

'Pity. Never mind. Another time,' the wolf said and watched Polly disappear up the road.

'I'm not going to make that disgusting stuff again. Chairs, that's what I need. Polly will come past my house, feeling very tired, and when she looks in and sees three chairs all empty and ready for her to sit on, she won't be able to resist coming in to try them out. I'll see what I can arrange to tempt her tomorrow,' the wolf said to himself.

It was not the next day, but a week later, that Polly was near the wolf's house again. She looked down the road and saw, not smoke this time, but a group of boys apparently reading something on his front door.

When she reached them, Polly saw a large sheet of paper fastened to the knocker, on which was written:

NOTICE

THERE ARE THREE CHAIRS IN THIS HOUSE

The boys were busy writing a message underneath.

So what? We've got four chairs and a put-U-up

The door opened suddenly, and the wolf bounced out.

'How dare you write on my door?' he shouted at the boys.

'Someone's been writing on it already,' one of the boys said.

'That doesn't mean you have any right to. Who wants to know that you've got a put-U-up?'

'Who wants to know you've got three chairs?' the boy answered.

'She does,' the wolf said, pointing with his head towards Polly.

'No, I don't.'

'Yes, you do. And one's too high, and one's too low, but the other's just right. Come in and try them,' the wolf said.

'I don't think I'd better,' Polly said.

'Yes, you'd better. It would be fun.'

'Not much. Not for me.'

'I'd enjoy having you,' the wolf said, and his long red tongue flicked out of his mouth for a minute. He laid a large black paw on Polly's shoulder and began to steer her in through the doorway.

'Why don't we all come in? Come on, boys,' Polly said, holding on to an arm she found near her.

'I asked you. I don't want all of them,' the wolf said, disgusted. But it was too late, the boys were already through the doorway and looking about the wolf's living room. There were indeed three chairs. The wolf had decided not to spend good money on buying anything new, but to adapt what he'd already got, to fit the story.

'Why is that chair on the table?' the smallest boy asked.

'To make it too high, of course. Stoopid!' the wolf replied.

'Stoopid yourself. Now no one can sit in it,' the boy said.

'Is this supposed to be a chair?' another boy asked. He was looking at what appeared to be a seat almost on the ground.

'That's the one that's too low. I chopped its legs off,' the wolf said, complacently.

'That's cruel. How would you like it if someone chopped your legs off?' the boy said.

'I'm not a chair. I'm a wo– I mean, I don't need to be made any lower. I'm the proper height for a . . . for the sort of person I am,' the wolf said.

'This one's all right,' a third boy said, sitting in the only other chair.

'You shouldn't be sitting in it. Polly's supposed to do that,' the wolf complained.

'That's all right. I'm not tired. Thank you very much for showing us your interesting furniture, but I think it's time we went home to our teas,' Polly said, moving towards the door.

'No, wait! You haven't tried all the chairs yet and said this one's too high and this one's too low and this one's all right and then you break it,' the wolf said.

'If she doesn't want to break it, I will,' the third boy said, and before the wolf could stop him, he had got out of the chair, picked it up by one leg and brought it down on the corner of the table with a crash which sent splinters of wood flying round the room. The little chair lay sadly on the floor; it had lost three of its legs and its back was broken. 'Like that?' the boy asked.

'You wicked boy! You've broken my only good chair! Go away and don't ever come back!' the wolf cried out. 'Not you, Polly. You stay here and I'll . . . I'll make some more porridge,' he said quickly.

'No, thank you, Wolf. I don't like porridge any more than you do.'

'But you haven't tried the beds!'

'You have three beds?' Polly asked. She knew now which story the wolf had been reading lately.

'Well, nearly three,' the wolf said.

'And one's too soft and one's too hard, but the other one is just right? And I'm supposed to try them all and then go to sleep in the little one?'

'That's right! You'd make a good detective, Polly.'

'Thank you, Wolf. Would you tell me how you've managed about the beds? To make one too hard and the next too soft?'

The wolf smirked. It was not a pretty sight. 'It wasn't easy, I can tell you. First of all, I put a lot of stones and some firewood into the big bed, under the bottom sheet. That'll be hard enough, I thought, and I tried it, and it certainly was. Then for the middling-sized bed that's too soft, I thought there isn't anything softer than feathers, so I ripped open my pillows and I've covered my settee with feathers. It's so soft you can't hardly breathe. You'll see, Polly, when you come upstairs to try.'

'So now you haven't any pillows?' Polly asked.

'I sacrificed them for a good cause,' the wolf said.

'What about the last bed? The really comfortable one?'

The wolf looked embarrassed. 'I've had some trouble with that. To start with, I haven't got any more beds, and it didn't seem worth buying a brand new one just for such a short time. I tried putting two chairs together, but that wasn't a great success. I kept on falling down between them whenever I tried to stretch out. Then I made a sort of nest on the floor, but it was distinctly draughty. I thought perhaps you'd be able to advise me, Polly. After all, you're the person who's going to find it so comfortable. I did wonder if you could go to sleep in the dirty linen basket . . .'

'Certainly not! I'm not dirty linen.'

'Perhaps in the bath? It's quite dry, I don't use it very often.'

'Not the bath. Even if it hasn't been used for months.'

'You're being very difficult,' the wolf sighed.

'And, Wolf, it's all very well to try to have three of everything, but there's one thing you haven't thought of that you can't have three of,' Polly said.

'No, there isn't. I had three bowls for the porridge, and three chairs – until that nasty child destroyed one. And I've nearly got three beds. There's the bottom drawer of my kitchen dresser, I could make that very cosy with a couple of dishcloths and an old towel. That would make three beds, wouldn't it?'

'But there's only one of you,' Polly said.

'Of course. I am unique!' the wolf said, proudly.

'There were three bears.'

The wolf looked at Polly. He hated to admit it, but it seemed to him that she was winning the argument again, just as she had always won all the arguments they'd ever had. At last he said, in a small voice, 'You mean, it doesn't work if there's only one of me?'

'That's right. Now if you had a wife to be Mother Wolf . . .'

'But I don't want a wife! I want a meal!' the wolf cried.

'. . . or a baby to be Little Wolf . . .'

'I've never liked cubs much. Noisy, rough little creatures. A baby would disturb my elegant bachelor life,' the wolf said.

'Then you can't expect me to be like Gold-ilocks and come in and eat your disgusting porridge and sit on your chairs and sleep in your dirty linen basket or your bath. Or even in a drawer,' Polly said.

'Is that your last word?' the wolf asked.

'Not quite. Don't read so many fairy stories, Wolf. Face real life instead. Whatever cunning plans you make to catch me and eat me, you are never going to succeed, because what you don't realize is that I'm Clever Polly and you are the . . .' But the wolf was looking so disappointed that Polly hadn't quite the heart to say what she really thought of his brains, so she ended her sentence, '. . . you are just a Unique Wolf.'

3. At the Doctor's

WHEN the wolf came into the doctor's waiting room, he saw that it was crowded. There were several old ladies and old gentlemen, who didn't interest him much.

'Too tough and stringy,' he thought. But there were other patients who looked much more promising. One mother had two toddling twins, another had a succulent looking baby, and a fat little boy who was running round and round the table made the wolf's mouth water and his eyes glisten. He hoped that all the older people would get in to see the doctor first. Then, when he was left alone with the children, he would have a chance to seize one of them and leave quickly before anyone noticed.

'I don't have to go in to see the doctor today. I can always come back next week for what I need,' he thought.

The mother with the juicy baby was called next, but to the wolf's disappointment she took the baby with her. Next, one of the old gentlemen left. The two old ladies went together. Then another old gentleman disappeared. Meanwhile, one of the twins had fallen asleep on a chair and, to the wolf's delight, its mother was the next to go into the surgery. She took the wakeful twin with her, but after a quick glance at the other, she left it sleeping.

The wolf got up and went over to the table. He pretended to be studying the books and magazines that covered it, picking them up one after another and turning the pages. Then he tucked one under his front leg and, as if by mistake, crossed the room so that he was sitting on the chair next to the sleeping twin.

The fat little boy who had been running round the room and falling over people's feet now stopped in front of the wolf.

'That's not your chair!' he said.

'It's not yours either,' the wolf said.

'You were sitting over there,' the fat little boy said, pointing.

'Yes, and now I'm sitting here,' the wolf said.

'Why?'

'So that I can look after this baby who's asleep,' the wolf said, seeing his chance.

'You aren't looking after it. Its mum told my mum to do that,' the little boy said.

'We can both look after it,' the wolf said.

'You don't look like someone who looks after babies.'

'Oh, but I am! I often look after babies. I'm very good at it. I look at them and wonder whether they'd be good to fry or . . . I mean, whether they're going to be good or if they're likely to cry. Things like that.'

'I don't believe . . .' the little boy had begun to say, when his mother called him. 'Bill! Come over here! It's our turn to go and see the doctor. Hurry, now, or we'll miss our turn.'

'Aha! My chance has come,' the wolf thought as he saw Bill and his mother leave the waiting room. He put out a paw towards the still sleeping twin, when its mother's arm came between them.

'It's all right, I'm back. Thank you so much for looking after her. It's difficult when you've got two at once, isn't it?' the twins' mother said, scooping up the spare twin, decanting it into a twin buggy which appeared from nowhere, and wheeling both babies briskly out of the waiting room.

Ten minutes later, the doctor's voice called, 'Mr Wolfe?' and the wolf reluctantly followed the white-coated figure along a passage to the surgery.

'Do sit down. New patient, I think. What seems to be the trouble?' the doctor asked, scribbling on a long white form in front of him.

'Trouble?' the wolf asked.

'WHAT DO YOU NOTICE WRONG?' the doctor said, very loudly and clearly.

'I'm not deaf!' the wolf said indignantly.

'I beg your pardon. I was asking you what seemed to be the trouble?' the doctor asked again.

The wolf did not know what to answer. Could he explain to this sympathetic doctor that the trouble was that he wanted to catch Polly and eat her? Or might this be misunderstood? He said, doubtfully, 'I have trouble with a girl. Quite a small one, but I can't seem to catch her when I want to.'

'A hyperactive child, perhaps?' the doctor asked.

'Uh?'

'She is too active for you? Never sits still? Talks too quickly and too much?'

'Much too much,' the wolf agreed, glad to be understood at last.

'Sleeps badly?'

'I'm not sure about that.'

'Is she aggressive?'

'Uh?'

'Aggressive. Fights with her mates. Won't do as she's told.'

'I don't know about her mates. She certainly never does what I tell her,' the wolf said.

'Argues a lot?'

'Never stops arguing. I can't tell you. Whatever I say or whatever I do, it's always talk, talk, argue, argue, till I don't know whether I'm standing on my head or my tail . . . my feet,' the wolf said.

'Is she in the waiting room? Let's have her in and I'll take a look at her,' the doctor said.

'No. You can't. She's not there. Anyway, what good would just looking at her do?' the wolf asked.

'Bring her in tomorrow, then. Anything else bothering you?' the doctor asked, in the sort of voice that means, 'I haven't got time to listen to you any more, you'd better leave.'

'I'm bothered about not getting enough to eat. I'm hungry!' the wolf said, hoping that this would make the doctor more sympathetic.

The doctor looked more interested. 'Unnatural appetite?' he suggested.

'Depends on what you mean by unnatural. It's quite natural for a wo– for the sort of person I am.'

'Three hearty meals a day, is that it?'

'When I get them,' the wolf said sadly.

'Good mixed diet? Plenty of veggies and fibre?'

'Veggies? Fibre?' The wolf shuddered.

'What, then? Convenience foods? Ready-made frozen stuff?'

'Meat,' the wolf said.

'Just meat? Nothing else at all? That's not what I call a healthy diet. Not to mention the expense.'

'I can eat cake. Polly once cooked a delicious cake,' the wolf remembered.

'Who is Polly? Never mind. What you need is an appetite depressant,' the doctor said, drawing his prescription pad towards him and beginning to scribble rapidly.

'A what?' the wolf asked, alarmed.

'Appetite depressant. Something to take the edge off your appetite so that you don't get these terrible feelings of hunger. And try to eat some fibre, there's nothing like it for filling the stomach. Good for the bowels too,' the doctor said.

'There's nothing wrong with my stomach. Or my bowels,' the wolf said, indignant.

'I'm surprised. Have this made up at the chemist, and come back and see me in a couple of weeks. And do, for goodness' sake, try to get down some bran or wholemeal bread for breakfast. And, by the way, if you'd like to bring your little girl, I might be able to suggest a diet which will quieten her down a bit. Next please!' the doctor said briskly, opening his door and bustling the wolf out.

'Bran! What does he think I am, a rabbit? Whoever heard of a wolf eating bran?' the wolf asked himself as he walked down the street towards the chemist. While he was waiting for his prescription to be made up, he passed a tempting-looking butcher's and nipped in just in time to secure a large piece of steak for his supper. He hadn't much faith in the doctor's advice for himself, but he decided that it would be worthwhile finding out what he might suggest to make Polly easier to catch.

It was nearly three weeks later that Polly saw the wolf waiting at the school gate at the end of the afternoon's lessons.

'Hi!' the wolf said as she came down the path.

'Hi, Wolf! What are you doing here?'

'Waiting for you,' the wolf said.

'I'm not going to walk home with you,' Polly said, remembering that there might not be many people about in the road where she lived.

'No, no. Of course not. That's not what I wanted to ask you.'

'What did you want to ask?'

'I wanted to tell you that I have consulted a very clever doctor.'

'Have you been ill? Poor Wolf!' Polly said, kindly.

'I have not been ill. I was consulting him about you.'

'But I haven't been ill either.'

'He says you are hyperactive.'

'No, I'm not! What's that mean anyway?' Polly asked.

'Means you can't keep still and that you talk too much and argue too much and run about too fast, and it isn't good for you.'

Polly began to understand what the wolf meant. She said, 'You mean I can run faster than you?'

'Only when I've just had dinner. Not now, this minute . . .'

'I'm not running. I'm staying here till my friends are ready to go home.'

'Ah. In that case . . . But no. I want to advise you about your diet.'

'You mean what I eat?'

'That's what diet means.'

'Go on, then. You can tell me, but I don't promise to do it.'

'This very clever doctor says you should cut out dairy foods.'

'What's that?'

'Milk. Cheese. Butter. Anything made with milk or cheese or butter. He says it will make you feel much better.'

'What about you, Wolf? Did he tell you what you should eat, too?'

'He was wrong,' the wolf said.

'What did he say?'

'He said . . . And I don't like bran and I hate vegetables.'

'What for? Why bran? Why vegetables?'

'To fill me up when I get hungry. Instead of . . .' The wolf stopped in the middle of his sentence. He did not mean to let Polly know that the doctor thought he ate too much meat. After all, what was Polly herself? Not bran. Certainly not a vegetable.

'Why didn't he tell you not to eat cheese and milk and all that?'

'I am not hyperactive,' the wolf said smugly.

'When he says hyper-whatever it is, he means clever,' Polly said.

'That's not what he said.'

'But he did say that talking and arguing a lot was hyper-something?'

'Ye-es.'

'Wouldn't you like to be clever, Wolf?'

'I am clever,' the wolf said.

'Clever-*er*, then? Cleverer than me?'

The wolf considered this. 'It might be an advantage, yes.'

'Then you ought to be eating all the things he said I shouldn't. Lots of butter and milk and cheese and cream. Then you'd always be able to run faster than me and you'd be cleverer than everyone else. That's sense, isn't it?'

The wolf thought about this for some time. It did seem sense. If those foods made Polly as quick and clever as she was, they ought to have the same effect on him.

'Why do you think the doctor told me to eat bran and vegetables, then?' he asked.

'Perhaps he guessed that you wanted to catch me to eat and he didn't like the idea,' Polly said.

'But that's unfair! It was me went to see him and asked for his advice! He ought to have been on my side!' the wolf cried.

'People are unfair,' Polly said, with feeling.

'He cheated me!'

'But anyway, now you know what to do,' Polly said.

'I'm going straight off to the dairy. I'm going to drink a pint of double cream and eat as much cheese as I can swallow. And next time we meet, stupid little Polly, you'll see, I shall run like the wind and my brain will be working so well it will dazzle you. As for you, you'd better go on my diet. Cabbages and bran. We shall meet again,' the wolf cried as he left the school gate and walked sedately down the road.

Polly looked after him. 'Oh, Wolf! You certainly aren't dazzling me with your cleverness yet,' she thought.

4. In Sheep's Clothing

THE WOLF stood in the school playground, waiting for the children to come out at the end of the afternoon. The parents, mostly mothers, who were waiting there too, looked at him suspiciously and none of them came over to speak to him. He was so very dark, so very hairy. None of them could remember noticing him there before.

Boys and girls began straggling out of the building. Some clutched large sheets of paper on which they had painted portraits of their families. Others carried egg-boxes, cardboard cylinders from used toilet rolls, empty cotton reels, shells, nuts, melon seeds and corks, from which they had made pretty and possibly useful gifts. For Christmas was coming, and the children in this school were encouraged to be generous with their time and ingenuity.

The wolf had to wait for what seemed a long time before he saw Polly in a group of children, talking excitedly. This lot carried something different. One child had a pair of large wings in her hand, two more had long, striped robes over their arms, and Polly was carrying a baby doll wrapped in a long white shawl.

'Hi, Wolf!' Polly called out when she saw him.

'Hi, Polly! What's that doll for? I thought you didn't play with dolls.'

'I don't. Not much. Anyway this doll isn't mine, she's Lucy's. I just borrowed her for the nativity play.'

'What sort of play?' the wolf asked.

'A nativity play.'

'What's that?'

'It's about the first Christmas. You know. Jesus being born in a stable and all that. We're acting it the day after tomorrow, and I'm going to be Mary. She's Jesus' mother. It's the best part.'

'A play! Couldn't I be in it too?' he said. Surely acting in a play with Polly and several other deliciously small children would give him a chance to get one of them.

'It's only for my class to act in. And there aren't any more parts to go round.'

'Who else is there besides Mary and that doll?'

'There's Joseph. Benjie is being Joseph. And there're some angels. Sophie over there is an angel. You can see her wings.'

'Why isn't she wearing them on her back if she's an angel?'

'She will when we act our play. There's an innkeeper, that's Michael. He has to say, "No room, no room." And then we go into the stable and I have the baby.'

'Anyone else?' the wolf asked.

'Three kings . . .'

'Couldn't I be a king? I'd be very good as a king,' the wolf suggested, rather fancying himself in a crown.

'No, you couldn't. Derek's one of them and the twins are being the other two. And Marmaduke's being King Herod, who's horrible and wants to kill all the babies.'

'To eat?' the wolf asked.

'I don't think so. And there are a lot of shepherds. They don't have much to say, so they're the children in my class who can't remember long speeches.'

The wolf had brightened at the sound of shepherds. 'Shepherds? With sheep?'

'I suppose so. But no one wants to act a sheep.'

'I would,' the wolf said.

'You? Be a sheep? But you're nothing like a sheep.'

'I could act like a sheep.'

Polly wasn't sure that he could. 'How?' she asked.

'Baaa. Baaa . . . aa. Baa . . . a . . . baa . . . a. Baa!' the wolf said loudly. Several of the parents standing in the playground turned round to look and one or two of them laughed.

'How was that?' the wolf said, pleased with the effect.

'It wasn't bad. But you don't look like a sheep.'

'I haven't dressed for the part yet. After all, when I came out this afternoon, I had no idea I might be asked to be in a play.'

'No one has asked you,' Polly said.

'So when is the performance, Polly?' the wolf went on, taking no notice of this remark.

'The day after tomorrow. Wolf . . . !' Polly began, but before she could finish the sentence, the wolf had gone.

'Benjie. Sophie. Marmaduke. Not to mention Polly. And a lot of shepherds who are too stupid to say anything. I ought to get one of them,' he thought as he trotted home.

When he got there, he went straight to his larder; this was something he always did, sometimes hoping that though he had left it nearly empty when he went out, it might miraculously have filled up in his absence. But the shelves were as bare as before. The wolf sighed, shut the larder door and walked into his sitting room where, on the floor, lay a not very clean, whitish-grey fur rug. It had belonged to the wolf's grandfather, and how he had got it it is probably better not to know. It was, in fact, a whole sheepskin, and it was the thought of this priceless possession that had made the wolf so confident that he could take part in Polly's nativity play.

For the rest of that day and for most of the next, the wolf practised. He practised with pieces of string and with safety pins and elastic bands. He even tried to sew with a needle and thread. For most of the time, he practised in front of his long mirror, and at last, on the very morning of the performance, he was satisfied. He not only sounded like a sheep, he now looked like one. After a light midday meal, he carefully dressed himself in his disguise and made his way to Polly's school, using side streets so as to avoid notice.

He managed to slink in at a back door. He heard a gabble of excited voices coming from a classroom further along the passage and, looking cautiously through a glass door, he saw a great many children dressed for the play. He saw a couple of angels in long white nightgowns and gauzy wings. He saw two kings, exactly like each other, wearing golden crowns. He saw several boys and girls in striped robes, with pieces of material wound round their heads. One of them carried a small stuffed lamb under his arm. So these were the shepherds, the wolf guessed. On the further side of the classroom, he saw Polly in a blue dress, with a blue veil on her head, holding the doll baby by one leg, upside down.

The wolf pushed the door open and joined the actors.

'Hey! Who're you pushing?' angrily asked a small stout king in a red robe edged with gold tinsel.

The wolf swallowed a snarl and the temptation to take a mouthful out of a plump leg very near to him, and said, 'I just want to get over to the shepherds.' He knew he would have to be careful until everyone was off their guard and thinking about nothing but the play. He did not want to make a disturbance, and he was particularly anxious that Polly should not see him yet.

'Timmy! here's one of your sheep!' the red king shouted.

'We haven't got any sheep,' a shepherd called back.

'There's one here. Don't know who. Miss Wright must've got someone in extra.'

Lucky, thought the wolf, that no one seemed surprised at this, and no one took any particular interest in him. He lay down under one of the tables pushed against the wall and amused himself by remarking which children were fatter or slower (or both) and so would be the easiest prey. After a short time he noticed that the teacher was looking over each child's costume, hitching up the wings on one angel, tying up Joseph's shoelaces (they came undone again a moment later) and taking the doll baby away from Polly-Mary. 'You don't have the baby in the first scene, that's when the angel comes to tell you you're going to have it,' she said, and put it on a chair.

'Now, we're all going into the hall. Very, very quiet, please. Sophie and Polly, are you ready for Scene One? The others can stand at the side and watch, but no talking and no fighting. Understand?' She gave the three kings a special glare, and led the way out of the classroom.

The wolf trotted quietly behind the children. Along one long passage, turn a corner, another passage, and then a swing door into the hall. People were singing. The wolf caught one or two words: '... midwinter ... snow ... snow ... long ago.' It sounded cold and disagreeable. Why not sing about something pleasant, like hot soup, a roast joint? Chips? He found himself jostled among the children and crowded into a small space at the side of the stage, with one of the kings leaning against his shoulder and a shepherd treading on a hind paw.

'I wish ...' So many juicy little arms and legs all round him. 'But I must wait. If I gave myself away now, I'd never get out of here alive,' he thought, and licked his chops silently.

The singing had stopped. The curtain was drawn back from the front of the stage, and the wolf heard, 'Hi, Mary. You're going to have a baby and it's called Jesus.'

'But I'm not even married!' Polly's voice answered.

'That doesn't matter, because it's God's baby,' the angel said, and walked off. Then Joseph walked on and told Mary they had got to go on a long journey. 'But I'm going to have a baby!' Mary said, and Joseph said, never mind that, she could have the baby in a hotel somewhere on the way.

'When do we get to the shepherds?' the wolf asked a child next to him in a loud whisper. He was bored with all this talk about the baby.

'Not till after the baby's got born, silly,' the child whispered back.

'No talking!' Miss Wright's voice hissed behind them, and the wolf had to wait while

Mary and Joseph were told that there was no room in the inn. 'But you can use the stable, if you like,' the innkeeper said kindly.

There was some more singing. The wolf was by now not only squashed, but also terribly hot. The children round him were all warm and excited and he was wearing an extra skin. An elastic band round one of his ankles was too tight, and a shepherd behind him was apt to tread on the fleshy part of his tail. It was a relief when Miss Thompson whispered, 'Go on, Timmy, it's the shepherds now,' and the group round the wolf moved out on to the stage.

The lights were bright here, and for a minute the wolf's eyes were dazzled. Then he saw Polly, in her blue veil, sitting on a stool, surrounded by bales of straw, with the doll baby on her lap. Joseph stood behind her. The shepherds moved towards her and the wolf followed them.

'Hullo, Mary. We heard about your baby, so we've come to have a look at him,' the largest shepherd said.

'You're welcome,' Polly said. She still hadn't seen the wolf.

'We've brought him some presents. Here's an apple,' one of the younger shepherds said, holding out the apple.

'Thank you. I'm sure he likes apples,' Polly said.

'And I've brought a lamb,' another shepherd said.

The wolf thought this was a good moment to give a loud *Baa . . . a . . . a*. Everyone jumped, and the child carrying the stuffed toy lamb said, 'You aren't supposed to say that.'

'Why not? I'm a sheep, aren't I? "Baa" is sheep language,' the wolf said.

'You didn't say that when we rehearsed yesterday,' the first shepherd said.

'I wasn't here yesterday. But I am today. Baa . . . aa,' the wolf said, annoyed.

'He's made me forget what I was supposed to say,' the smallest shepherd said, and burst into tears.

'It doesn't matter, just go on. Thank you for the lamb, it will be nice for Jesus to play with when he's older,' Polly said, quickly.

'You're not the lamb I'm giving Jesus, this is,' said Timmy, showing the toy lamb.

'I don't think he's a lamb at all. He's got black paws,' another shepherd said.

'Some sheep do have black feet. And black noses,' the wolf said.

'He's got a long black tail that sticks out behind, too,' the second shepherd said.

'I haven't! Have I?' The wolf tried to look over his shoulder. There was a tearing sound and the wolf was aware that the fleece was slipping badly and a large safety pin at the back of his neck had come open.

'I don't think he's a sheep either,' Joseph said, interested, and coming round to look.

'I'm not! I'm a wo–' the wolf began, but Polly interrupted. 'Of course he's a sheep. He came in with the shepherds, didn't he? And he's wearing a sheep's coat.'

'Polly, you know who I am. Tell them,' the wolf complained.

'Children, get on with the play, it's time you made room for the kings,' Miss Wright hissed from the side of the stage.

'I expect you want to get back to watch your flocks by night,' Polly said politely to the shepherds, who began to shuffle towards the way out. To the wolf she whispered, 'You stay here. And don't forget, you chose to be a sheep in this play, now you've got to act like one.'

'You mean I've got to go on saying "Baa"?'

'That's right. Just "Baa" and nothing else.'

'Don't I get anything to eat?'

'Sheep eat grass. I don't think there is any grass round here. There's a little straw if you'd like that.'

'Don't sheep eat meat ever? Not a mouthful of leg?' the wolf asked, gazing at the fat little leg of one of the three kings who were now preparing to offer their gifts to the baby Jesus.

'Certainly not! Thank you very much, that'll make a nice smell in this stable,' Polly said to the third king, who had just given her a box supposed to contain myrrh.

'But I'm not an ordinary sheep. And I'm hungry!' the wolf said, rather too loud. The fat-legged king turned round and said, 'Shh! It's my turn to talk now. We're going home without seeing Harold again because we know he means to try to kill your baby. That's all. Bye-bye.'

'Who's Harold?' the wolf asked, wondering whether this was someone who shared his taste in food.

'Herod, not Harold. Don't talk, Wolf. You're not supposed to say anything but "Baa".'

'But that's silly.'

'Sheep are silly. If you wanted to do something clever, Wolf, you ought to have acted a different part.'

'So I've got to go on being a silly sheep and I can't catch anyone? Not even you?'

'I'm afraid so. I'm sorry, Wolf. Joseph and I have got to go now. But you can stay for a bit and go on being a sheep, if you want to. Until we've all gone home, then you can go back to being a stup– to being a wolf again. Come on Joseph, it's time we went to Egypt,' said Clever Polly, and left.

5. You have to Suffer in Order to be Beautiful

THE WOLF stood in front of his long mirror and looked at himself all over.

'Nothing wrong there. Long legs, lean, healthy body, kind, intelligent face. No two ways about it, I'm a good-looking fellow,' he thought. He pulled in his stomach and bent a front leg to make the muscles stand out. 'And I'm not really overweight. I've got big bones, that's all.

I've been making a mistake. I shouldn't have told Polly that what I really want is to eat her. I should have pretended that I admired her. In stories, the girl always falls for the man who says he wants to marry her . . . Ugh!' The wolf shook his head. 'Why are they always so keen on marriage? But if I pretended to want to marry Polly, then when I'd got her home with me . . . Yes, that's it! I shall woo her. After all, it wasn't always handsome young princes those girls fell for. Look at Beauty and the Bea–. Well, Polly isn't exactly Beauty, so she can't expect to get a Prince.'

'Yes, Mr Woolf. And may I ask how you came to hear of me?' the immensely smooth, pink-cheeked doctor asked the wolf, who was sitting on the opposite side of an elegant desk in a consulting room in a private health clinic.

'I saw your advertisement . . .'

'I never advertise. It is not allowed in medical practice,' the doctor said, displeased.

'I read something in the newspaper that said you could work miracles. Make people look different.'

'Perhaps miracles is a slight exaggeration. But certainly many of my clients tell me that they are very happy with what I am able to do for them. So what can I do for you?' the doctor asked.

'It's a very delicate matter,' the wolf said.

'Ah! Perhaps you have some special reason for coming to see me at this moment in time?' the doctor suggested.

'Yes, I have. A very special reason.' Because if I look quite different, and Polly doesn't recognize me, I'll have a better chance of catching her, had been the wolf's clever idea.

'An affair of the heart, perhaps? There is some girl you wish to approach? But so far, you have not dared?'

'I can dare, all right. But she won't listen to me.'

'You wanted to make some changes to your appearance?' the doctor asked.

'What sort of thing do you suggest?' the wolf asked.

68

'Well, for instance, noses. Not everyone is satisfied with the nose they have. I can alter a nose to almost anything you might require. Roman? Snub? Classical? Short and appealing? Long and learned? Now in your case, Mr Woolf, I should suggest a certain curtailing . . .'

'Doing what? My tail's all right,' the wolf exclaimed in alarm.

'Curtailing. Shortening. It has no effect on the olfactory function, I assure you.'

'Olfactory?' the wolf asked.

'You'll be able to smell with it as well as before.'

'So I should hope! If I couldn't smell, I might just as well not have a nose,' the wolf said.

'Then there are teeth. I work in conjunction with a first-class dental surgeon. Now it seems to me that your teeth leave quite a lot to be desired. If you'll forgive my saying so, they are on the large side and a little discoloured. It happens in later life, you know.'

'Later life! I'm in my prime!' the wolf said, angrily.

'Of course. I did not mean to imply . . . But you might like to consider a really good set of dentures. Something smaller and whiter. I assure you, it would have a really dramatic effect on your general appearance.'

'Dentures? What are dentures?' the wolf asked.

'New teeth. Fitting perfectly so that there would never be any danger of them slipping and so causing you unnecessary embarrassment,' the doctor said.

'You mean false teeth?'

'Exactly. Dentures.'

'Would they be able to gnaw bones?'

'Certainly.'

'And chew up a juicy little gir–, a juicy little Pol–, juicy little anything?'

'They would function perfectly,' the doctor said.

'He's awfully difficult to understand. It must be being so clever makes him use all these long words,' the wolf thought. Aloud he said, 'I'm not sure about false teeth. I'll think about it.'

The doctor looked him over carefully. 'Then, if you don't mind my suggesting it, we might tackle the problem of superfluous hair.'

'What's that?' the wolf asked, puzzled again.

'Superfluous hair. You are more bountifully endowed with hair than most of us.' The doctor himself, indeed, was almost completely bald. 'We could tackle that with electrolysis, though I must warn you that it would take time.'

'What do you want to do with my hair?' the wolf asked, not having understood a word of this last sentence.

'Remove it. Not all of it, of course. Just some around the upper part of the face, to give you a more open, friendly expression.'

'I've got a friendly expression,' the wolf said.

'Of course, Mr Woolf. Delightful expression. But a *leetle* difficult to see with that very luxuriant growth of hair over the forehead and cheeks. I can't help feeling that this young woman you are interested in might respond to – shall we say, a less hirsute approach.'

'Her suit? Or my suit? But I haven't got one!' the wolf cried, thoroughly confused by all this language.

'She might like you better without so much hair,' the doctor said, annoyed at having to use ordinary words.

'What was that word you used about my hair?' the wolf asked.

'Superfluous. Means you have too much of it,' the doctor said.

'Not that one. Electro something.'

'Electrolysis. It is a means of eliminating super– unwanted hair, by the insertion of an electric needle into each hair root . . .'

'Sounds uncomfortable. Does it hurt?' the wolf asked.

'Only for a moment,' the doctor assured him.

'And that gets rid of the lot? All in a moment?'

'No, no, Mr Woolf. Each individual hair has to be dealt with separately.'

'Wow! And these extra teeth? I suppose it doesn't hurt to have another set to put in when you need them?'

'Having first extracted the original dentition.'

'Uh?' said the wolf.

'First of all, we take out everything you've got there.'

The wolf shuddered.

'What about the nose job?'

'That necessitates a few days in hospital while we break down the bones of your face and construct a totally new form. Sometimes we have to take a little skin from a leg or arm in order to cover the new nasal apparatus.'

'Take skin from whose leg or arm?'

'Yours, of course, Mr Woolf. It is a perfectly simple procedure.'

'I'll think about it,' the wolf said. He did not mean to think about it at all. He saw that all these operations were going to hurt a lot, and he did not mean to suffer that much even in order to catch stupid little Polly.

'My secretary will see you on your way out,' the doctor said, rising from his chair and shaking the wolf's paw rather coolly. He did not believe that this client was likely to come back to ask for a complete reconstruction of his appearance, however much he wanted to get his girl.

'That will be one hundred and fifty pounds, Mr Woolf,' the charming secretary said, as the wolf passed through her office.

'A hundred and fifty? Pounds? You must be joking!' the wolf snorted.

'Will it be cash or a cheque?' the charming secretary asked.

'I haven't got my cheque book on me just now,' the wolf said. This was not surprising, as he did not have a cheque book anywhere.

'Perhaps you could drop a cheque in the post this afternoon?' the secretary said.

'Perhaps,' the wolf said, and left. 'A hundred and fifty pounds, for threatening to break the bones in my face, skin my leg, take out all my teeth and electrocute my fur? The man's a monster!' the wolf thought as he hurried down the street.

*

'Polly,' the wolf said, looking over the fence into Polly's front garden, where she was lazily swinging herself in the sun.

'Yes, Wolf?'

'Would you like me better if I didn't have so much hair . . . fur?'

'Bald all over, d'you mean? No, I wouldn't. I think you'd look terrible,' Polly said.

'Suppose I had an extra lot of teeth? False ones?'

'What for? You've got enough, haven't you?'

'Or if I had my nose shaped differently?'

'But you wouldn't look like a wolf if you had a different nose,' Polly said.

'But would you like me any better?'

'No. I like you just as you are,' Polly said, quite affectionately.

'Wonderful! Then come with me, Polly. Now! To my home. Make me the happiest of . . . wolves.'

Polly laughed. 'No, thank you, Wolf. I like you a lot, but I don't trust you for a minute.

I like you where you are now – on the other side of the garden fence. And like a wolf, not with your long nose made short or with all your teeth pulled out. Just go on being yourself, and I'll stay like I am. Safe,' said Clever Polly.

6. Kind Polly and the Wolf in Danger

THIS STORY is different from all the other stories about Polly and the wolf, because it doesn't start with the wolf planning how he can have Polly to eat.

One day, Polly went out to do some shopping for her mother in the village. She had bought a cauliflower and some potatoes at the vegetable shop, and a pound of sugar and half a pound of biscuits at the grocer's, and she was thinking of going home again, when she heard a loud noise coming from a side street.

She ran to the corner and looked along the street and saw a crowd of people all very angry about something. The people were shouting and someone was howling. Polly thought that she knew that howl, and she hurried up the street.

As she got nearer the crowd, she could hear more distinctly what the people were saying.

'Ought not to be allowed!'

'Would worry the sheep!'

'Cause a dog fight!'

'Steal a hen!'

'These beasts are dangerous. Should be behind bars!'

'Might bite a baby!'

'Could easily kill a child!'

'Someone muzzle it!'

'Someone shoot it!'

Polly began to believe that she knew whom the voices were talking about, but she still hadn't managed to get through the crowd to see if she had guessed right. Now she heard other voices saying other things.

'Interesting shape. Don't know if I've ever seen one exactly like that before. A new breed, perhaps?'

'Look it up in the *Gazette*.'

'Like to have a look at its bones. Preserve the skeleton in formaldehyde . . .'

'Curious sound it makes. Don't know if I've ever heard a dog howl exactly like that . . .'

Polly pushed through the inner ring of trousers and skirts and saw a wooden tea chest set up on end. Out of the top of the tea chest stuck the head of the wolf, and over this head, someone had thrown a net, which was held down by the edges of the chest. The wolf was in a bad way. His fur was draggled, he was trembling and he was looking this way and that with huge, terrified eyes.

'It'd make a splendid exhibit for the local museum. Stuffed, of course,' a large man in a tweed jacket was saying. Polly saw a glimmer of hope cross the wolf's face, and she realized that he was thinking of being stuffed as an agreeable sensation after a large meal. But the hope disappeared the next moment, as a woman added, 'You have to be careful how you kill an animal you want to stuff. A bullet through the heart is fine, but whoever shoots must know how to be accurate.'

'I'm against killing. This animal should be in a zoo,' another woman said.

'Doesn't look in very good shape to me. Death might be a mercy,' a man said.

'Shouldn't be shot, though. Call in the local vet.'

'Spoilsport! Why not have a chase? We could get the hounds. Creature would enjoy a good run for its money,' said another voice.

'Cruel! I object! No blood sports here!' said someone else.

'In any case its body should be preserved for expert examination.'

'Call the police!'

'Send for the Master of the Hunt!'

'Fetch my gun!'

The voices grew louder and more quarrelsome. Everyone seemed to be shouting at everyone else. Polly managed to edge closer. 'Wolf!' she said.

The wolf turned his miserable eyes towards her.

'You here?' he said.

'What happened? Why are they all so angry? What did you do?'

'I didn't do anything,' the wolf said sullenly.

'I don't believe that. Tell me the truth.'

'I didn't do anything out of the ordinary. I've seen plenty of people do it.'

'Go on.'

'I've often seen people go round sniffing at other people's babies.'

'Sniffing at them?' Polly asked, surprised.

'Bending right over their prams, with their noses in the children's faces. And you can hear them smacking their lips.'

'Probably kissing them.'

'Nonsense! Sniffing to see if they're ready to eat. Smacking their lips when they know what a good meal they're going to have.'

'Is that what you did?' Polly asked.

'Only one or two. The first was a scrawny little thing, not worth its salt. The second wasn't any good, either. It hit me. I did not hit back. Naturally I didn't want a struggle.'

'And then?'

'Then I saw exactly what I needed. Small, plump, juicy-looking. Not unlike you, a few years ago. I was just unwrapping it, to make sure it was perfectly fresh, when this woman came dashing out of the shop and started screeching and calling me all sorts of names, and then a couple of men came up and got hold of my legs, and they held my jaws so that I couldn't speak, and they pushed me into this revolting box and covered me with a net.'

'Oh Wolf! What did you expect? Had you forgotten that people don't eat babies?'

'I can't think why not. There seems to be a very good supply,' the wolf said.

'Would you eat wolf cubs?'

'Certainly. If I was hungry.'

'Well, most people don't eat babies. So when they saw you sniffing into prams, they realized that you weren't a human. They knew you were a wolf.'

'No, they don't. They don't know what I am. Didn't you hear what they said? They think I'm very unusual,' wolf said, with a little pride.

'Don't be too pleased about that. It's because you're so unusual that they want to dissect you.'

'What's dissect?' the wolf asked.

'Cut you up to find out how you work.'

'Cut me up alive!' the wolf cried.

'Not alive. Dead.'

'Cut me up, dead?'

'Or shoot you and stuff you. Not with food. With cotton wool, or whatever you stuff dead creatures with,' Polly explained.

The wolf shuddered.

'Or they might want to hunt you. With dogs.'

'What am I going to do?' the wolf said, and at his howl, several people in the crowd turned round to see what was happening.

'Don't stand so close, little girl. That animal is dangerous,' a man in spectacles said.

'I've met him before,' Polly said.

'Then you know that he is a threat to our community,' Spectacles said.

Polly thought quickly. 'I'll tell you what I do know. He's a very strange animal. There's never been anything quite like him here before.' (*That's true enough*, she said to herself.) 'In fact he's Unique.'

'I am NOT,' she heard the wolf mutter behind the net, but she took no notice and went on.

'You know what a fuss everyone makes about not letting rare kinds of plants and animals disappear. I can tell you, if you hurt this animal, there's going to be a terrible fuss. You'll get blamed by everyone important. The

Queen will be angry, and the Prime Minister will be furious, and I wouldn't wonder if the whole village didn't get punished.'

There were murmurs among the crowd. They were obviously impressed. She heard, 'Seems to know what she's talking about.' 'Don't want the place to get a bad name.' 'Remember what the Green Party said on television the other night, about preserving the balance of Nature.'

'I expect one of the television stars would tell everyone what a terrible thing had happened here,' Polly said, reminded of the power of TV.

'She's right. We don't want to be held up to scorn as vandals,' the tweedy man said.

'Animal Rights,' said a thin woman who hadn't spoken before.

'I still think it should be put behind bars. In a zoo,' said a fat man.

'Polly! I won't go into a zoo,' the wolf said in an undertone.

'Can't I have it to keep in my room?' a small boy asked his mum, who said, 'Sorry, sweetie, I don't think Dad would like it.'

'That wouldn't be too bad,' the wolf said, looking over the small boy hungrily.

'He shouldn't be in a zoo. He should be allowed to roam free,' Polly said.

'Not around our village!' someone said quickly.

'Where he belongs. In forests, or on hills. Wherever he came from,' the thin woman said.

'Where did you come from, Wolf?' Polly asked, wondering why she had never asked this question before.

'Can't remember. I didn't come out of a box, I do know that.'

'In fact, he's almost certainly one of an endangered species,' Polly said.

'I don't! I wouldn't, anyway, if you let me go!' the wolf cried.

'Wouldn't what?' Polly asked.

'Make dangerous speeches. It's not the sort of thing I do.'

'I didn't say speeches, I said . . . what that means is that you're very special and we ought to take great care nothing terrible happens to you.'

'Now that makes sense . . . Why don't all the other . . .' the wolf began, but he was interrupted by the man in spectacles, who had raised his hand and said, 'Ahem! Ahem! It seems to me that we should take a vote on the question of what to do with this . . . this . . . unusual animal. I for one am not prepared to take the responsibility of advising its destruction . . .'

'What's that?' the wolf whispered to Polly.

'Killing you,' Polly whispered back.

'. . . by whatever means. The choice therefore lies between sending it to one of the many zoological institutions in this country, or, as my friend here has suggested, letting it go free to its natural habitat . . .'

'Natural what?' the wolf wanted to know.

'Where you live, Wolf.'

'. . . wherever that may be. Could we have a show of hands, please? Those wishing the animal to go to a zoo put up their hands.'

He counted. 'Four . . . six . . . Are you holding up your hand, Madam, or adjusting a hatpin? . . . Seven . . .'

'Wolf! If I loosened the net here, could you creep out?' Polly whispered. She had discovered that she could pull the edge of the net a little away from the bottom of the tea chest.

'If I make myself very thin.'

'And if I do, will you promise . . . ?' But Spectacles had now finished the first count and there were too many people looking round. Polly waited till she heard the second counting begin. Then she finished the sentence. 'Will you promise not to try to catch me to eat ever again?'

'Of course. I promise. Now let me out,' the Wolf said, far too quickly.

'You didn't mean that. Think about it.'

The wolf thought. 'You mean really, truly, never?'

'Really, truly, never.'

'But it's been fun! Hasn't it?'

'Sometimes. Frightening, too.'

'Being frightened is fun. And anyway, you're so clever, Polly. You've always managed to escape up till now.'

'You've never said I was clever before,' Polly said.

'I didn't realize how clever you are till I heard you say that about dangerous speeches,' the wolf said.

Polly was pleased. She began to say, 'Well, just promise . . .' But the sentence never got said, for at that moment the wolf, seeing that she wasn't thinking about holding the net as tightly as before, pushed his head up and pulled it out of her hands. There was a bump, a crash, and a moment later, the wolf was out of the tea chest, free of the net, and was streaking down the High Street, terrifying passers-by and only just avoiding cars and bicycles.

Luckily no one blamed Polly.

'But I wonder what he thinks his natural habitat is? I'm sure it's not forests or hills, it's much more likely to be this village where he knows his way around,' she thought and wondered if she would ever see him again. Probably. He wasn't likely to give up now that on this occasion it had been the wolf who had flattered and fooled her. Clever Polly had for once met a not-so-stupid wolf.

Extra!

Extra!

READ ALL ABOUT IT!

CATHERINE STORR

MORE STORIES OF CLEVER
POLLY

1913	Born Catherine Cole on 21 July in Kensington, London
1924–31	Catherine is a pupil at St Paul's Girls' School in London where she is lucky enough to be taught by Gustav Holst, the music teacher at the school, learning to play the piano and the organ, eventually becoming the organist for the daily morning service at the school
1931	Catherine is accepted at Newnham College, Cambridge, where she studies English literature
1937	Catherine writes her first children's story, Ingeborg and Ruthy. Ruthy was the name of her much-loved doll as a child
1940	Ingeborg and Ruthy is published by George G. Harrap & Co. Catherine returns to

Cambridge to study medicine. At Cambridge she meets and falls in love with Anthony Storr, a fellow medical student

1942   *Catherine and Anthony marry*

1944   *Catherine and Anthony qualify as doctors. Both also start training in psychiatry. Catherine gives birth to the first of three daughters*

1950–63 *Catherine works part-time as a senior medical officer in the Department of Psychological Medicine at the Middlesex Hospital and also writes stories for children. As her daughters grow older, she writes books for older children*

1952   *Her first two books are published:* Stories for Jane *and* Clever Polly, and other stories

1955   Clever Polly and the Stupid Wolf *is published and becomes hugely popular*

1957   *A sequel,* Polly and the Wolf Again, *is published*

1958   Marianne Dreams, *a novel for older children, is published. It has remained in print ever since and has been published in many foreign languages*

1960   Marianne and Mark *(the sequel to* Marianne Dreams*) is published*

1961   *Catherine helps to set up the Charlotte M. Yonge Society, devoted to studying the Victorian*

novelist who was a bestselling author of her time

1966	*Takes on a new job as an editor at Penguin Books and continues writing*
1971	Thursday, *a novel for young adults, is published*
2001	*Catherine dies aged eighty-seven on 8 January in London; her last book is published in the autumn*

INTERESTING FACTS

First published in the 1950s, the Polly and the Wolf stories have remained in print ever since, and published in many different languages in countries around the world.

When she was young Catherine Storr liked to create her own make-believe world with her dolls, and it was her favourite doll, Ruthy, which inspired her first book for children, Ingeborg and Ruthy.

ABOUT THE ILLUSTRATOR

JILL BENNETT

Jill Bennett was born in Johannesburg, South Africa, in 1934. She began drawing from an early age and always wanted to be a children's book illustrator. She also loved the theatre and studied at Wimbledon School of Art, specializing in Theatre Design, and the Slade School of Fine Art. Jill went on to illustrate many wonderful children's stories by authors such as Roald Dahl and Dick King-Smith.

Jill is also the creator of exquisitely detailed miniature dolls that have been displayed in museums all over the world.

INTERESTING FACT

Jill was the first illustrator of Roald Dahl's *Fantastic Mr Fox* and later *Danny the Champion of the World*.

WHERE DID THE
STORY COME FROM?

Catherine's daughter – the real Polly – says:

'*My sisters and I were very lucky that our mother,
Catherine Storr, had a wonderful imagination and the
desire to be a writer. Our childhood was full of stories
told or read to us. When I was five or six my family visited
Whipsnade Zoo which had a wood where wild wolves
lived. I remember looking through the chain-link fence
into the dark wood and seeing wolves slinking through the
trees like ominous shadows. I was very frightened by the
wolves, and my fears continued after we returned home.
So my mother wrote a short story for me called "Clever
Polly" in which Polly avoids a wolf's efforts to eat her by
outwitting him. This story was the first of many more
about Clever Polly and the Stupid Wolf.*'

WORDS GLORIOUS WORDS!

*Lots of words have several different meanings – here are a few you'll find in this Puffin book. Use a **dictionary** or look them up online to find other definitions.*

insulted   *offended by someone being rude or disrespectful*

necessitates   *requires someone to do something*

dentition   *the type, number and arrangement of a set of teeth in humans or animals*

bachelor   *an unmarried man*

vandals   *people who deliberately cause damage to other people's property*

complacently   *being pleased or satisfied with oneself*

GUESS WHO?

A 'No two ways about it, I'm a good-looking fellow . . .'

B 'I can alter a nose to almost anything you might require. Roman? Snub? Classical? Short and appealing? Long and learned . . .?'

C 'You know we don't allow pets in the classroom. Your dog must go home. Immediately!'

D She had discovered that she could pull the edge of the net a little away from the bottom of the tea chest.

ANSWERS: A) *The wolf* B) *The doctor* C) *Miss Wright*, *the teacher* D) *Polly*

DID
YOU
KNOW?

A *male* wolf is called a dog, a *female* is called a bitch and the *young* are called pups.

The scientific name for wolf is *Canus Lupus*, and they are members of the *Canidae* family, which includes dogs and foxes.

Wolves *communicate* with each other by *howling*. The sound of a wolf howl can be heard up to a *mile* away.

Wolves can run as fast as *35 miles per hour* when they are hunting.

QUIZ

Thinking caps on –
Let's see how much you can remember!
Answers are at the bottom of the opposite page.
(No peeking!)

1 **In 'The Wolf at School' what country does the teacher believe the wolf is from?**

a) *Germany*

b) *Hungary*

c) *Italy*

d) *Norway*

2 **What story had the wolf been reading in 'Thinking in Threes'?**

a) *The Three Little Pigs*

b) *The Three Billy-Goats Gruff*

c) *Goldilocks and the Three Bears*

d) *The Three Sillies*

3 *What does Polly make the wolf promise never to do again?*

a) *To try and catch her to eat*

b) *To follow her into school*

c) *To dress up as a sheep*

d) *To pick her mother's tulips*

4 *Why does the wolf go to see the doctor?*

a) *For a diet plan*

b) *For some cough medicine*

c) *For advice on how to catch Polly*

d) *For an appetite depressant*

5 *What part is the wolf given in the school Nativity Play?*

a) *The Sheep*

b) *The Donkey*

c) *The Shepherd*

d) *The King*

MAKE AND DO

More yummy than porridge!

The wolf hates porridge so perhaps he'd like to try this delicious crunchy granola instead – it's full of healthy ingredients (it might even tempt Polly!).

Ask an adult to help you set the oven to 180°c/350°F/Gas Mark 4

YOU WILL NEED:

* A large baking tray
* 300g jumbo rolled oats
* 100g mixed seeds (e.g. sunflower, pumpkin, sesame)
* 100g flaked almonds

* A handful of broken nuts, such as walnut pieces
* 120g golden syrup
* A squeeze of runny honey
* 1 teaspoon of vanilla essence
* Handful of dried fruit, such as raisins, cranberries or chopped apricots

1 Put all of the dry ingredients except the dried fruit in to large bowl.

2 Stir the golden syrup, honey and vanilla essence into the oaty mixture until everything is lightly coated.

3 Tip the mixture on to the baking tray and spread out roughly with your mixing spoon.

4 Place the tray in the oven and bake for about 20 minutes until the mixture is crunchy and golden brown.

5 Ask an adult to remove the tray from the oven. Allow the mixture to cool and then break it up into small pieces.

6 Stir in the dried fruit and store in an airtight jar for you, Polly (and the wolf, if he's good) to enjoy!

CATHERINE STORR

MORE STORIES OF CLEVER
POLLY
AND THE STUP'D
WOLF

The legendary leader **Nelson Mandela** *is released from prison in South Africa. He becomes President of South Africa in 1994.*

The Simpsons *is shown on US television and becomes an instant hit.*

The **Hubble Space Telescope** *is launched.*

Tim Berners-Lee, an English computer scientist, begins his work on the **World Wide Web.**

The two halves of the **Channel Tunnel** *are joined together for the first time when rail construction workers from* **England** *and* **France** *complete their digging 40 metres below the English Channel.*

PUFFIN
WRITING
TIPS

Ask: who, what, where, when, why and how? It'll help you dig deeper and find out more about your characters.

If you have enjoyed *More Stories of Clever Polly and the Stupid Wolf* you may like to read even more of their adventures in *Tales of Polly and the Hungry Wolf* . . .

2. The Great Eating Competition

'I DARE you!' the wolf said loudly. He had to speak loudly, because he and Polly had met in the High Street on a Saturday morning, and there were plenty of other noises, over which he wanted to make himself heard. Cars were grinding up the hill, horns were blowing, motorbikes were revving, children were calling, babies were yelling and people were shouting so that their friends could hear what they were saying.

'What do you dare me to do?' Polly shouted back.

'A trial of strength. A trial of something or other. You know the sort of thing. We could try which of us could lift the heaviest stone.'

'There aren't any heavy stones around here,' Polly said, looking up and down the High Street.

'We could try that lady. I'm sure she weighs as much as a really large stone.' The wolf pointed a paw towards a very large lady, just about to go over a zebra crossing.

'I wouldn't try to lift her, if I were you. If you did, she'd probably call the police and have you put in prison.' Polly wasn't sure whether or not the wolf might have been able to lift the lady, but she was quite sure that she herself would not be able to.

'Oh, all right. You suggest something, then,' the wolf said, sulkily.

'Shall we see who can talk the fastest?' Polly asked.

'That's mean! You know you'd win that. Not because I haven't got plenty to say, and very well worth saying too. But because I like to think before I speak.'

'I've read a story where the people tried to see who could tell the biggest lie,' Polly said.

'I am shocked. I am horrified. I thought you were a good, truth-telling girl,' the wolf said primly. He spoiled the effect by asking quickly, 'What did they say? What was the biggest lie?'

'I meant a made-up story. Like someone saying he'd taken a bite out of the moon,' Polly said.

'Really? That would explain a lot. I have often wondered why the moon so often seems to have suffered from some sort of attack. Sometimes from one side, sometimes from the other. Often you can see just where someone has taken a bite out of her. I never knew that before,' the wolf said, considering the matter.

'But I didn't mean that that was true. I meant, that was the sort of story someone might make up.'

'But why should he say so if it isn't true?'

'To see if anyone else could think of a bigger lie,' Polly said.

'Easy! Anything would be a bigger lie than saying that there is someone taking bites out of the moon. You can see that it's true every now and then, by just looking at her.'

Polly felt unable to go on with the subject. It was obviously not going to be possible to convince the wolf that someone was not regularly taking mouthfuls of moon. She waited for his next remark.

'I'll tell you what. Suppose we have a competition to see which of us could eat up the other one fastest,' the wolf said.

Polly thought about this. She was puzzled. 'How would that work?' she asked.

'Simple. Simple to anyone with any brains, that is. Suppose I start eating you at, say, ten o'clock this morning . . .'

Polly looked at the clock tower. The clock showed that it was now a quarter to ten.

'We have an umpire, with a watch. I eat as fast as I can, and when I have finished, snap, gobble-you-up, crackle, crunch, I tell him so. He looks around to make sure that there's nothing left that could reasonably be considered eatable. I shouldn't be eating your clothes, you know, Polly. I should kindly leave them for you or another little girl to use again.'

'But they wouldn't be much use to me if you'd eaten me all up,' Polly pointed out.

The wolf took no notice of this and hurried on. 'So, I tell the umpire. He looks at his watch and he sees that I have taken exactly forty minutes. Fifty perhaps. It would depend on how tough you had turned out to be, and on other details which I won't mention just now. Then the umpire announces that I have won. Easy!' The wolf sounded very much pleased with himself.

'What happens when it's my turn to eat you up?' Polly asked.

'It would take you far longer than forty or fifty minutes to eat me. It might take you hours. Possibly even a whole day. I am larger than you. I am exceedingly tough. And then there's the hair,' the wolf said.

'What about hair?'

'Hair is a great slower-down of fast eating. Hair in the wrong places can make a quick snap almost impossible. I mean in the wrong places for a mouthful, of course. Naturally for a wolf it is right and proper to have hair all over. A great deal of hair, covering most of his body. While you are very nearly quite bald. Your hair all grows in one place, on top of your face. It would be easy to get rid of it in five minutes or so, while it would take you several hours to get rid of mine, I reckon,' the wolf said with pride.

'But if it had been me that started, you wouldn't have had a chance to try. I would have eaten you first.'

'That's why I should start. After all, as we know that I could eat you faster than you could eat me, there wouldn't be any point in your trying.'

'But that wouldn't be fair!' Polly exclaimed.

'Life is not fair. Some people are born as wolves, others are only feeble little girls. Some people are born with brains. Others are stupid from the beginning. There's nothing you can do about that.'

'You can do something about trying to make a competition fair,' Polly said.

'What do you mean? You couldn't make yourself eat twice as fast, could you? Only it would have to be more like a hundred times as fast.'

'I don't think anyone could make me eat that much faster. But they could make you eat more slowly. That's what they do when there is a horse-race,' Polly said.

'Do you have races where horses eat each other? I never knew. I'd like to see that.'

'Don't be disgusting, Wolf. They don't eat each other. They gallop. The horse that gallops fastest wins the race. If one horse is much faster than the others, it has to carry a heavier weight than the others. They fasten pieces of lead to its saddle, to slow it down,' Polly said.

'How monstrous! Poor horse. Terribly unfair.'

'No, it isn't. It makes the race fairer for the other horses. The slower ones have a chance to win.'

'Now, let's stop thinking about boring things like galloping horses. Let's talk about us,' the wolf suggested.

Tales of Polly and the Hungry Wolf
is available in A Puffin Book.